P9-CRA-688

Daddy Calls Me Man

A RICHARD JACKSON BOOK

Daddy Calls Me Man

by ANGELA JOHNSON

paintings by
RHONDA MITCHELL

ORCHARD BOOKS

NEW YORK

Text copyright © 1997 by Angela Johnson
Illustrations copyright © 1997 by Rhonda Mitchell
First Orchard Paperbacks edition 2000

Orchard Books, A Grolier Company, 95 Madison Avenue, New York, NY 10016

Manufactured in the United States of America
Printed and bound by Phoenix Color Corp.
Book design by Jennifer Browne

Hardcover 10 9 8 7 6 5 4 3 2
Paperback   16   16 17 18/0

The text of this book is set in 24 point Aldus.
The illustrations are oil paintings on canvas reproduced in full color.

Library of Congress Cataloging-in-Publication Data
Johnson, Angela.
Daddy calls me man / by Angela Johnson ; paintings by Rhonda Mitchell.
p.   cm.
"A Richard Jackson book"—Half t.p.
Summary: Inspired by his family experiences and his parents'
paintings, a young boy creates four poems.
ISBN 0-531-30042-0 (tr.)   ISBN 0-531-07175-8 (pbk.)
[1. Family life—Fiction. 2. Afro-Americans—Fiction. 3. Paintings—Fiction.]
I. Mitchell, Rhonda, ill. II. Title.
PZ7.J629Dah 1997 [E]—dc21 96-53865   40

To my loving grandmother,
Mattie Bell Floyd
—A.J.

To Him from whom all blessings flow.
Thanks for everything.
—R.M.

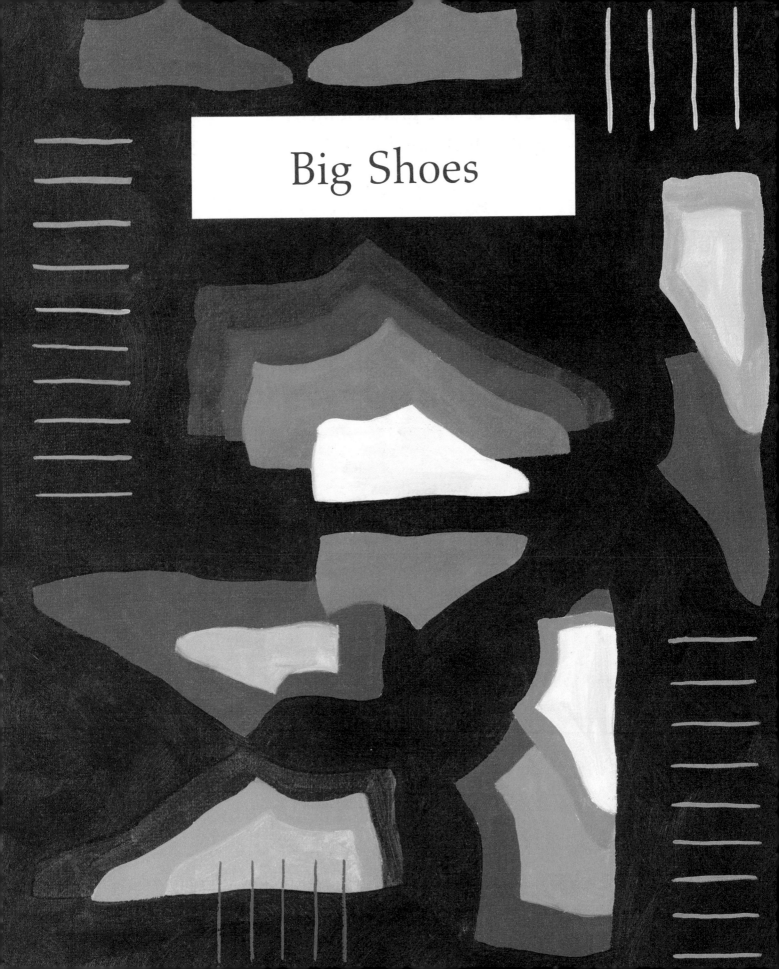

Big Shoes

All I want is big shoes

Tie shoes

Fast shoes

Red and black jump high shoes.

Line them up by Daddy's

and call them all our shoes.

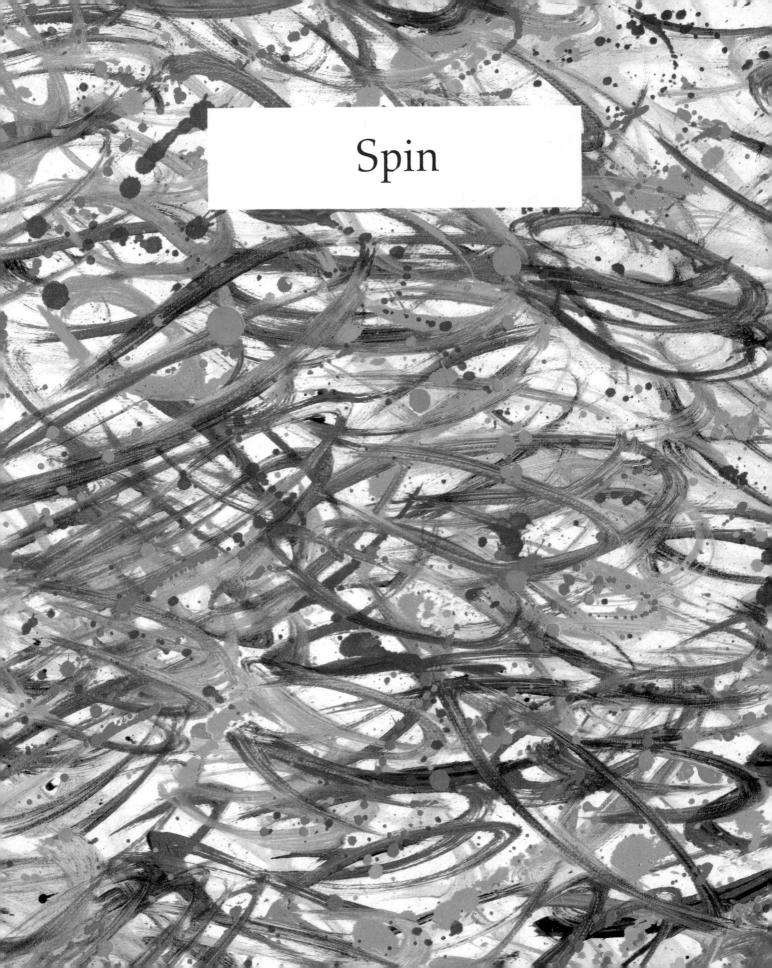

Spin

Spin around the room.

Spin around the tree.

Swirl

Twirl

Spin and twist

Big sister and me.

Noah's Moon

Mama calls it Noah's moon and says
it lives glowing in the sky.

Half a moon
Full moon

Me asking why.

Full moon, half moon
Glowing in the sky.

Baby Sister

Got a new baby sister
everybody comes to see.

Little bitty fingers
and smiles just for me.

I share toys
my room
and JoJo
anytime I can.

Then Mama calls me sweetheart

and Daddy calls me man.